MAKE BA
CELEBRATE

MRS BUN THE BAKER

Mrs Bun the Baker®

HELLO

There are quite a few celebrations during the year and to include them all would be impossible! In this book I recognise celebrations from January to December and all around the world. If you have a celebration coming up, hopefully I can help you with a recipe to suit the occasion.

There are 33 recipes (a few sweeter than savoury) but a good mixture of them. Some of the savoury you can make as a sweet, and some sweet you can make as a savoury!

In the book you will find most recipes have variations so you don't just have 1 recipe it could become 2 or 3 more! With the variations in the book there are around 100 recipes!

Each cake recipe in the book can become a birthday cake, after all some of us like a chocolate cake, others a fruit, lemon, or a plain sponge. There are breads to bake, pasta and pastry to try too. Something for everyone!

Every recipe has been tried and tested at both the Bun HQ cookery school and by all the wonderful people who have joined my face to face or online classes. As well as the free Friday bake alongs during the lockdown of 2020/21 when we had people from all over the world join us!

Most recipes can be made within the hour and you can just use your table-top, which means it can be baked in an oven or kept cold in the fridge. However, there are a few recipes that do require the use of the hob. These are highlighted with the hob icon – ,so do please look for this and check the hob safety guide opposite when using it.

I hope you enjoy the recipes just as much as my classes have, but don't just save them for these occasions, make them at other times of the year too. Soon you will be making your own variations!

Mrs Bun the Baker

BEFORE YOU BAKE

Wash your hands: you and your food want to be clean!

Aprons: they keep you clean.

Hair: tie it back if it is long; hairs in food are not hygienic or acceptable.

Surfaces: give them a good wipe down before you start with a clean cloth, you don't know what was on there before!

EQUIPMENT

Most of the equipment needed should be found in your cupboards at home, from bowls, jugs, spoons to baking trays and bun tins. You will, of course, need a good set of scales for weighing ingredients, no guess work please or else those cakes and biscuits will turn out very different.

HOB SAFETY GUIDE

- Always use a wooden spoon or heatproof spatula with the saucepan; a metal spoon will conduct heat and make your hand very hot.
- The hob ring must not be bigger than your pan; you will feel the extra heat which could burn you.
- Never set the heat too high unless I have said to boil it. You will burn the food in the saucepan.
- Do not look over the saucepan if there is oil in it, in case it 'spits' at you.
- Always turn the hob off when you have finished.
- Make sure saucepan handles do not stick out-so they don't get knocked off the stove.
- Children must always have an adult to help them.

TIMING

Timings given in the recipes are only a guide – every oven is different. Some may be hotter at the back or the side. Some are electric, fan or gas, so please use the times, but adjust them up or down to suit your oven.

RECIPES

BUN
MAKE
BAKE

J

3 KINGS BREAD

3 KINGS DAY

Whilst living in Spain, Mr Bun and I were lucky enough to have an extra holiday on the 6th of January – 3 Kings Day. More food! Celebrations! And presents! This bread was just delicious.

INGREDIENTS ▸ MAKES 1 LOAF

DOUGH

- **75g BUTTER**
- **50g SOFT BROWN SUGAR**
- **1 ORANGE and 1 LEMON**: zested
- **2 EGGS**
- **150ml MILK**: warmed
- **475g PLAIN FLOUR**
- **7g or 1 SACHET YEAST**: fast action

FILLING

- **25g BUTTER**: melted
- **150g MIXED PEEL**
- **150g GLACE CHERRIES**: chopped
- **100g SULTANAS**: optional
- **1 EGG WHITE**: for glazing
- **25–50g FLAKED ALMONDS**: optional
- **MARZIPAN SHAPES**: optional

HOW TO MAKE

1. PREPARATION

Preheat the oven to gas 4 or 180c (fan 160c).

Line a baking tray with greaseproof paper.

2. FLAVOUR BUTTER

Place the butter into a bowl and squish and squash it down with a spoon, so it is lovely and soft.

Add in the sugar, orange and lemon zests and mix well.

3. CRACK THE EGGS

Crack the eggs into a jug and add to the butter.

Pour in the warmed milk and mix it all together.

4. COMBINE

Tip the flour and yeast into a bowl.

Add in the warmed milk mixture with the flavoured butter.

Stir them together with a spoon until all the flour is mixed in, then bring it together with your hands.

TIP: The dough will be a little soft.

5. KNEAD & ROLL

Knead the dough on the worktop for 5 minutes.

Place it back in the bowl, cover with clingfilm and leave the dough to prove for 45–60 minutes (it will double in size).

6. SHAPE & MAKE

Once the dough has proved, squash and squeeze the air out that has been created.

Sprinkle the worktop with some flour and place the dough on top.

Sprinkle a little more flour over the top and roll the dough out into a rectangle 60 x 20cm.

TIP: Make fingerprints in the dough, then use your rolling pin to iron them out and watch the dough grow!

7. PAINT

Paint the melted butter over the rectangle.

Sprinkle over half of the mixed peel, half of the cherries and all of the sultanas if using.

8. ROLL UP! ROLL UP!

Take the longest side and tuck it in slightly and start rolling it up.

You should have a long Swiss-roll or sausage shape. Place it on a baking tray, bringing the ends together to make a circle.

Leave to prove for 45–60 minutes.

9. BAKE

Brush all over with the egg white and place the remaining fruit and flaked almonds over the top in a pattern.

Place in the preheated oven for 20–25 minutes until golden brown. It should feel hollow at the bottom when tapped.

Once out of the oven decorate with marzipan shapes, if using.

Circle

Pattern

Slice

J F M A M J J A S O N D

OATCAKES

BURNS NIGHT

The 25th of January celebrates the poet Robert Burns and his contribution to Scottish culture. He wrote Auld Lang Syne, which is a popular song at midnight on New Year's Eve!

INGREDIENTS ▸ MAKES 10–15

75g PORRIDGE OATS

75g PLAIN FLOUR

1 SPRIG FRESH ROSEMARY: chopped
or 1–2 TEASPOONS DRIED PARSLEY

25g CHEDDAR CHEESE: grated

60ml WARM WATER

1 TEASPOON OLIVE OIL

HOW TO MAKE

1. PREPARATION

Preheat the oven to gas 5 or 190c (fan 170c).

Line a baking tray with greaseproof paper.

You will need a 5–6cm round cutter.

2. DRY

Place the oats into a blender and whizz up into a fine powder.

Add in the plain flour, fresh rosemary or parsley and grated cheese.

Use your hands to mix it all together.

3. WET

Run the tap until you have some warm water.

Measure 60ml of water into a jug and add in the oil.

Pour the water and oil into the dry mixture and mix well with a spoon. Then use your hands to squeeze the dough into a ball.

The dough should be quite firm, not crumbly or sticky.

TIP: If the dough is too dry, dip your hand in some water and squeeze it into the dough. If it's too wet, add some flour.

4. **BISCUIT MAKING**

Flour the worktop and split the dough into 4 pieces.

Place 1 piece on the flour and sprinkle some flour over the top.

Very gently roll this piece out to the thickness of a pound coin.

Take your cutter and cut out your rounds.

Add your leftovers to 1 of the other 3 pieces, roll out again, and keep repeating the process until you run out of dough!

Place the shapes on a baking tray.

TIP: You can put the rounds close together as they don't spread.

5. **BAKE**

Place in the preheated oven for 15–25 minutes (smaller ones will cook quicker).

They will turn a light golden colour and firm to the touch.

Take out and leave to cool on the baking tray.

Serve with butter, cheese or paté.

VARIATIONS

Add some paprika or chilli instead of the herbs.

Instead of cheese, add some pumpkin or sunflower seeds.

Use wholemeal flour instead of white flour.

Use oatmeal instead of porridge oats.

J F M A M J J A S O N D

CHOCOLATE MUFFINS

VEGANUARY

January is Veganuary. This recipe is from Grandma Bun; it's light, moist and tastes lovely. No one would ever guess that there was no egg in the muffins!

INGREDIENTS ▸ MAKES 12

FUDGE ICING

- 2 TABLESPOONS COCOA POWDER
- 50g MARGARINE
- 200g ICING SUGAR: sieved
- 4 TABLESPOONS OAT/SOYA MILK

MUFFINS

- 50g COCOA POWDER
- 250g SELF-RAISING FLOUR
- 125g CASTER SUGAR
- ½ TEASPOON BICARBONATE OF SODA
- 250ml OAT/SOYA MILK
- 100g MARGARINE
- 50g GOLDEN SYRUP
- 1 TEASPOON VANILLA ESSENCE

HOW TO MAKE

1. PREPARATION

Preheat the oven to gas 4 or 180c (fan 160c).

You will need a 12 holed muffin tin and paper cases to fit.

2. FUDGE ICING

Measure the cocoa, margarine, icing sugar and milk into a heatproof bowl and place in the microwave for 20 seconds, keep doing this in short bursts until it has melted together.

Pour the mixture into a bowl and place it in the fridge to set.

TIP: If you have no microwave, place the ingredients in a saucepan and melt on a low heat.

3. MUFFINS

Add the cocoa into the flour.

Sift them into a bowl, so they mix together well.

Stir in the sugar.

4. DISSOLVE

Place the bicarbonate of soda in a cup.

Add a tablespoon of milk from the 250ml and stir.

Leave to one side.

5. MELT

Put the margarine, golden syrup and the rest of the milk in a heatproof bowl.

Place the bowl in the microwave for 30 seconds, or until the ingredients have melted together.

6. COMBINE

Time for a spoon. Pour the melted ingredients over the dry ingredients and stir them together.

Add the vanilla essence and bicarbonate of soda mixture to the cake batter and mix all together.

Using a tablespoon divide the mixture equally between the paper cases.

7. BAKE

Place in the preheated oven for 17–20 minutes.

Leave to cool.

Place a spoonful of the fudge icing on the top!

VARIATIONS

Add orange zest for a chocolate orange flavour.

Make a mocha cake: replace a spoon of cocoa with coffee but dissolve it in some milk and add with the bicarbonate of soda.

J F M A M J J A S O N D

SCALLION PANCAKES

CHINESE NEW YEAR

New Year in China is celebrated for 16 days! It varies when it starts depending on the lunar calendar. Red and gold are the colours to wear. Each year one of 12 different animals is celebrated. Do you know what the 12 animals are?

INGREDIENTS ▸ MAKES 3

150g PLAIN FLOUR

80–90ml HOT WATER

4 SPRING ONIONS

CHINESE 5 SPICE

OIL: for frying

HOW TO MAKE

1. PREPARATION

You will need a frying pan.

2. MAKE THE DOUGH

Place the flour into a bowl.

Pour most of the hot water in, and stir with a spoon to make a dough. Add more water if it's too crumbly.

TIP: Don't add all the hot water unless you need it, otherwise you will end up with a soggy dough.

3. KNEADING

Knead the dough for 8 minutes.

TIP: You may need a little flour on the table, if it is a little sticky.

Once kneaded leave to one side to rest.

4. SNIPPING

Using a knife slice the spring onions open, lengthways, so you have '8' spring onions.

Use scissors to cut the spring onions into smaller pieces.

TIP: The spring onions need to be cut very small, to stop the dough breaking when making up the pancakes.

5. ROLL OUT & FILL

Break the pancake dough into 3 even pieces.

Sprinkle some flour on the worktop.

Place a piece of dough on the top.

Sprinkle some more flour over the top.

Roll the dough out to a circle of 20cm.

TIP: When rolling, keep turning the dough round so it doesn't stick to the table. Sprinkle some flour under the dough if it starts to stick.

Sprinkle over some Chinese 5 spice and a third of the spring onions, making sure you cover the whole circle.

6. ROLL UP, ROLL UP

Roll the circle up into a tight swiss roll.

Then roll it up so it looks like a snail's shell.

With your rolling pin, flatten the shell shape into a 15cm circle. You may need a little flour.

Repeat this with the other 2 pieces of pancake dough.

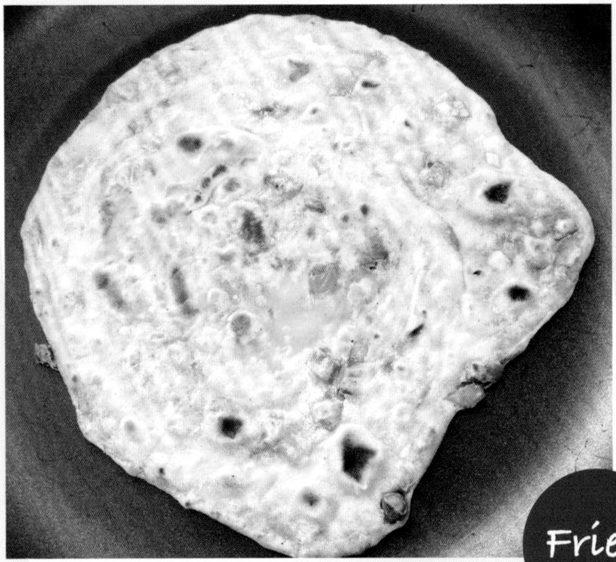

Fried

7. FRY

Pour a tablespoon of oil into a frying pan.

Place a pancake in the oil and fry each side on a low heat for a couple of minutes until speckled brown.

Try dipping your pancakes into sweet chilli sauce.

VARIATIONS

Double the recipe to make more.

Leave out Chinese 5 spice if you don't like it.

Sweeten them up and use sugar not spice and grated chocolate instead of spring onions.

Spread with chocolate chips or biscoff spread.

J F M A M J J A S O N D

HEART CAKE

VALENTINE'S DAY

Celebrate love and romance on the 14th February with this surprise heart cake!

INGREDIENTS ▸ 10–12 SLICES

CHOCOLATE CAKE

- 100g MARGARINE
- 100g CASTER SUGAR
- 75g PLAIN FLOUR
- 75g SELF-RAISING FLOUR
- 2 EGGS
- 2 TABLESPOON MILK
- 1 TABLESPOON COCOA POWDER

VANILLA CAKE

- 150g MARGARINE
- 150g CASTER SUGAR
- 3 EGGS
- 150g SELF-RAISING FLOUR
- 1 TEASPOON VANILLA ESSENCE

HOW TO MAKE

1. PREPARATION

Preheat the oven to gas 4 or 180c (fan 160c).

You will need a 16-18cm lined square tin or traybake for the chocolate cake.

You will need a lined 2lb loaf tin to combine the chocolate and vanilla cakes.

Small heart cutter.

2. CHOCOLATE CAKE

Place all the ingredients into a bowl and mix together with a spoon or electric whisk.

Pour the cake mix into the lined tin.

Place in the preheated oven and bake for 20–25 minutes, leave to cool.

3. VANILLA CAKE

Use the same mixing method as for chocolate cake.

Do not cook the cake!

4. CUT HEARTS

Take the chocolate cake out of its tin and cut heart shapes from the sponge and leave them to one side.

5. MAKE

Place a couple of tablespoons of the vanilla cake mixture at the bottom of the loaf tin.

TIP: You need enough mixture for the hearts to stand on.

Place the chocolate hearts all in a row, down the middle of the loaf tin.

Using a teaspoon, place the vanilla mixture around the sides and top of the chocolate hearts. Continue to fill the tin with the rest of the mixture.

6. BAKE

Place in the preheated oven for 45–60 minutes.

Leave to cool.

VARIATIONS

Try making a Christmas version with a tree shape, a ghost for Halloween, an egg for Easter etc...

J F M A M J J A S O N D

PANCAKES

SHROVE TUESDAY

Celebrating the feast day before the start of Lent, which is the 40 days leading up to Easter. This is Grandma Bun's foolproof recipe. Every Pancake Day these are made. We make our batter at lunchtime ready for teatime pancake flipping.

INGREDIENTS ▸ MAKES 4–6

100g PLAIN FLOUR

1 EGG

275ml MILK

BUTTER: for frying

HOW TO MAKE

1. PREPARATION

You will need a frying pan and a jug.

2. MAKE THE BATTER

Place the flour into a jug.

Crack the egg into a cup – make sure there is no shell.

Pour the egg into the flour and give it a whisk.

Add in the milk – slowly, whisking all the time to make a smooth batter.

TIP: The batter is better if you have time to let it sit for a while in the fridge.

3. PANCAKES

Melt a little butter in a frying pan on a low heat. Pour in some batter to thinly cover the bottom of the pan.

Leave it to cook on one side for 2–3 minutes.

Shake the pancake to see if it will move. Yes? Then turn it over with a spatula or have a flip of your pancake.

Cook the other side for another 1–2 minutes, until golden.

Serve with:

- Sugar and lemon
- Cheese
- Maple syrup
- Chocolate sauce
- Jam
- Ham and cheese

J F **M** A M J J A S O N D

WELSH CAKES

ST DAVID'S DAY

Celebrate the patron saint of Wales on the 1st of March. David was a teacher and a preacher, famous for his phrase 'Gwnewch y pethau bychain mewn bywyd' ('Do the little things in life').

INGREDIENTS ▸ MAKES 12–20

- 200g SELF-RAISING FLOUR
- 100g BUTTER
- 3 TABLESPOONS CASTER SUGAR
- 100g SULTANAS
- 1 TEASPOON MIXED SPICE
- 1 EGG

HOW TO MAKE

1. PREPARATION

Preheat the oven to gas 5 or 190c (fan 170c).

Line a baking tray with greaseproof paper.

You will need a 5–6cm round cutter.

2. MAKE THE DRY MIX

Place the flour into a bowl.

Chop the butter into cubes and add it to the flour.

Pick up some flour and butter and rub it between your fingertips (as though you are trying to get rid of something that's stuck). Keep rubbing your fingertips like this until the mixture looks like breadcrumbs.

Stir in the sugar, sultanas and mixed spice.

3. CRACK, MIX

Crack the egg into a cup and beat with a fork.

Make sure there is no shell!

Pour it into the dry mixture and mix well with a spoon.

Bring the dough together with your hands.

TIP: If it is a little dry add some milk, too wet add some flour.

4. ROLLING & CUTTING

Sprinkle some flour onto the worktop. Place the dough on top. Sprinkle some more flour over the top of the dough.

TIP: Don't drown the dough in flour; it is just a sprinkling.

Roll the dough out to ½cm thickness. Cut out your Welsh cakes.

TIP: Always start at the edge of the pastry when cutting, keep close to each round so you get out as many circles as possible.

Squeeze the leftovers together and keep rolling and cutting until all the leftovers are used up.

5. BAKE

Place them in the preheated oven and bake for 12–15 minutes.

VARIATIONS

You can cook them on the hob. Just melt some butter in a frying pan and cook each side of the welsh cakes for a couple of minutes, for a crispier outside and softer centre.

Replace the sultanas for chocolate chips. If you do this it is a good idea to chill the dough before rolling out, so the chips don't melt too much.

J F **M** A M J J A S O N D

SODA BREAD

ST PATRICK'S DAY

The 17th of March – celebrating the patron saint of Ireland and the introduction of Christianity to the island in the 5th century.

INGREDIENTS ▸ MAKES 1 LOAF

225g PLAIN FLOUR

50g PORRIDGE OATS

½ TEASPOON BICARBONATE OF SODA

6 SUN DRIED TOMATOES: chopped

100ml NATURAL YOGHURT

100ml MILK

HOW TO MAKE

1. PREPARATION

Preheat the oven to gas 6 or 200c (fan 180c).

Line a baking tray with greaseproof paper.

2. MAKE THE DRY MIX

Place the flour, oats and bicarbonate of soda into a bowl, and mix together with your hands.

3. FLAVOUR

Add in the chopped sundried tomatoes.

Mix so the tomatoes are all covered in flour.

Measure the yoghurt into a jug. Pour in the milk and stir together with a spoon so they're combined.

4. COMBINE

Pour the yoghurt mixture into the dry ingredients and mix well with a spoon.

TIP: The mixture may feel a little 'wet' this is fine.

5. BAKE

Scoop the mixture onto a floured worktop and knead gently to form a round and place on a baking tray.

Mark a cross in the top with a knife and place in the preheated oven for 20–25 minutes.

TIP: Once cooked the bottom should feel hollow when you tap it.

VARIATIONS

Instead of sun dried tomatoes use rosemary, olives, pumpkin seeds or cheese.

Make 5–6 small ones. Just use a spoon to scoop the dough onto the baking tray – it will be less messy on your hands.

MOTHER'S DAY LOAF

This day varies around the world but, in the UK, we celebrate it in the Spring. Treat your mum or someone special to this cake which is utterly delicious! I should know!

INGREDIENTS ▸ 10–12 SLICES

- 150g MARGARINE
- 100g CASTER SUGAR
- 3 EGGS
- 225g SELF-RAISING FLOUR
- 50g CRÈME FRAICHE
- 50g LEMON CURD
- 100g FROZEN FRUIT: blackberries, raspberries, blueberries

HOW TO MAKE

1. PREPARATION

Preheat the oven to gas 4 or 180c (fan 160c).

You will need a 2lb loaf tin, lined with greaseproof paper.

2. CREAM

Place the margarine into a bowl then squish and squash it down with a spoon, so it is lovely and soft.

Add the sugar and mix these together until they stick to the bowl.

TIP: If you can hold the bowl upside down over your head, without the mixture falling out on you, you have creamed it enough.

3. CRACK THE EGGS

Crack the eggs into a jug and beat with a fork.

TIP: To crack the egg, tap it lightly on a table. If it's not cracked, have another go, but not too hard!

4. MIX

Pour both the eggs and flour into the margarine mixture and mix it all together.

Add the crème fraiche and stir in.

5. FLAVOUR

Soften the lemon curd a little with a spoon and stir it into the mixture.

Add in ¾ of your chosen fruit and gently mix.

Pour the mixture into your loaf tin and scatter the remaining ¼ of fruit over the top of the loaf.

6. BAKE

Place the loaf tin in the preheated oven and bake for 50–65 minutes.

VARIATIONS

Use natural yoghurt, double cream or sour cream instead of crème fraiche.

If you don't like lemon curd, leave it out and add 25g more sugar to the recipe.

Serve with double cream.

Use chocolate chips instead of fruit and a swirl of chocolate spread instead of lemon curd.

Use different fruits according to the season.

J F **M** **A** M J J A S O N D

FISH PIE

GOOD FRIDAY

Traditionally, fish is served on Good Friday. Here is my simple recipe with no need for a roux sauce and all in the oven too.

INGREDIENTS ▸ SERVES 3–4

2 SPRING ONIONS

1 MEDIUM CARROT: cooked

2 BROCCOLI FLORETS: cooked

50g FROZEN PEAS

1 TIN of TUNA: drained (145g)

1 TIN of SALMON: drained (105g)

150g FULL FAT CREAM CHEESE

75ml MILK

2–3 SPRIGS of PARSLEY

100g CHEDDAR CHEESE: grated

SEASONING

1 PACK of READY ROLLED PUFF PASTRY

HOW TO MAKE

1. PREPARATION

Preheat the oven to gas 5 or 190c (fan 170c).

You will need an ovenproof dish (20 x 15cm).

You will need a 2–3cm cutter.

2. CHOPPING

Use scissors to cut up the spring onions. Chop the carrots up into small circles. Cut the broccoli up into small pieces.

Place all of these ingredients into a bowl.

Add in the peas and the drained tuna and salmon.

Stir it together with a spoon.

3. SAUCE

Place the cream cheese into a jug. Use a spoon to soften it slightly.

Pour the milk in slowly, mixing it with a fork so it isn't too lumpy.

4. ADD THE PARSLEY

Pull the leaves off the parsley sprigs.

Rip these leaves into small pieces and add them into the sauce mixture and stir.

5. COMBINE

Pour the sauce over the vegetables and tuna.

Add in the grated cheese.

Give it a really good stir. Season with some salt and pepper.

6. ADD THE TOP

Pour the mixture into your ovenproof dish and spread it evenly.

Unroll the puff pastry. Place it onto a floured surface. Use the cutter to cut out small circles and layer them all over the top of the mixture.

7. BAKE

Place in the preheated oven for 25–30 minutes.

VARIATIONS

Use sweet potatoes on the top, either mashed or sliced – they give a lovely colour and a lighter taste.

Swap the pastry for cooked pasta and make a fishy pasta bake.

Use potatoes, and sprinkle with some breadcrumbs to give a crispier topping.

Try a seafood version by adding cockles, mussels and prawns-a real taste of the seaside.

Use a flavoured cream cheese such as chive and onion or garlic to add some extra flavour.

M A

SIMNEL COOKIES

EASTER

These cookies are derived from my favourite choc chip cookie recipe and have all the goodies from a simnel cake in them. Utterly moreish and won't last the day!

INGREDIENTS ▸ MAKES 12

- 100g MARGARINE
- 75g SOFT BROWN LIGHT SUGAR
- 1 TABLESPOON GOLDEN SYRUP
- 75g MIXED DRIED FRUIT
- 25g MARZIPAN: optional
- 25g GROUND ALMONDS
- 1 ORANGE: zest
- 150g SELF-RAISING FLOUR

HOW TO MAKE

1. PREPARATION

Preheat the oven to gas 4 or 180c (fan 160c).

Line a baking tray with greaseproof paper.

2. CREAM

Place the margarine into a bowl and soften with the back of a spoon.

Add in the sugar and mix until it sticks to the bowl.

Pour in the golden syrup and mix it into the margarine and sugar.

3. FLAVOUR

Add the mixed dried fruit and stir into the margarine mixture.

Grate the marzipan straight into the mixture and mix well.

TIP: If you grate the marzipan on a board, it clumps together, so grating it straight into the bowl makes it separate into the biscuit mixture.

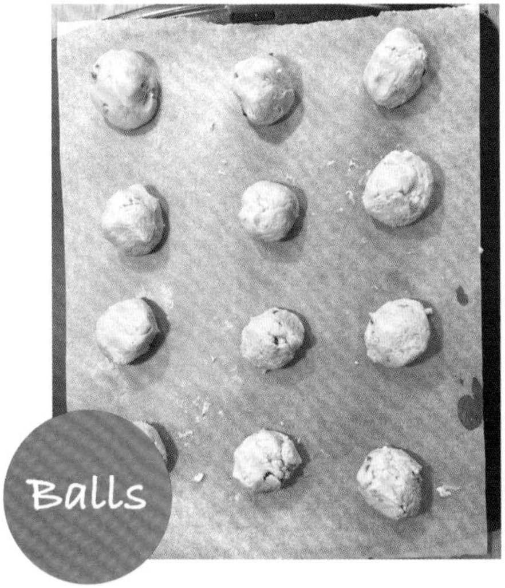

Stir in the ground almonds and the orange zest.

TIP: You will only have around a teaspoon of zest – a little goes a long way – it is full of flavour.

4. **FLOUR**

Using a tablespoon add the flour spoon by spoon. Make sure you add it all!

Give the mixture a good stir making sure all the flour has disappeared.

TIP: If the mixture is too sticky add a tablespoon of flour. Too dry add a drop of milk.

5. **MATHS**

Cut the ball of dough in half, and then in half again – you now have 4 pieces the same size.

Break each of the 4 pieces into 3 equal pieces – now you have 12 pieces of dough.

Roll the 12 pieces into balls.

Place the balls on a baking tray.

TIP: Make sure there is some space between them as they will spread out in the oven.

6. **BAKE**

Place in the preheated oven for 15–18 minutes until golden in colour.

Leave them to cool on the tray for 5–10 minutes.

VARIATIONS

Use caster or granulated sugar instead of brown sugar.

If you have mini eggs at Easter, crush those up and use 100g instead of the marzipan and fruit mixture.

If you don't like almonds, leave them out and add an extra 25g flour.

Use honey, maple syrup, agave nectar or date syrup instead of the golden syrup.

J F M **A** M J J A S O N D

CARROT MUFFINS

INTERNATIONAL CARROT CAKE DAY

Celebrating the lovable carrot on the 4th of April since 2003! The festival has grown and grown and now covers purple, white and any other colour of carrot! This is also Son Bun's favourite cake.

INGREDIENTS ▸ MAKES 6

- 2 EGGS
- 125ml SUNFLOWER or VEGETABLE OIL
- 75g SOFT BROWN SUGAR
- 75g CARROT: grated
- 75g SULTANAS or CHOPPED WALNUTS
- 125g SELF-RAISING FLOUR
- 1–2 TEASPOONS MIXED SPICE
- 200g FULL FAT CREAM CHEESE
- 1 ORANGE: zest
- 2–3 TABLESPOONS ICING SUGAR
- CHOCOLATE: grated

HOW TO MAKE

1. PREPARATION

Preheat the oven to gas 4 or 180c (fan 160c).

You will need a 6-holed muffin tin and paper cases to fit.

2. WET

Crack the eggs into a bowl; make sure there is no shell!

Pour the oil into the eggs.

Add the soft brown sugar.

Give the mixture a good whisk.

3. FLAVOUR

Add in the grated carrot.

Then add the sultanas or walnuts and mix with a spoon.

Lastly, add in the flour and the mixed spice.

Give these ingredients a good mix, until they're all combined.

4. BAKE

Divide the mixture between your muffin cases.

Place the muffins in the preheated oven for 25–30 minutes.

5. ICING

Whilst the cakes are baking, prepare the icing.

Place the cream cheese into a bowl and add the orange zest, mix well.

Add a couple of spoons of the icing sugar.

TIP: If it is lumpy icing sugar, then sift it into the cream cheese.

Have a taste test; if you would like it a little sweeter add another spoon of icing sugar.

6. DECORATE

Once the muffins are out of the oven, leave to cool.

Spread the icing over the top and sprinkle grated chocolate on the top.

TIP: If you have some carrot tops, place them in the grated chocolate to look like carrots growing.

TIP: If you have orange fondant icing, roll and flatten pieces the size of a 2 pence piece round, stick some parsley in it and you have made carrot tops!

J F M A **M** J J A S O N D

SUN SHINE CAKE

MAY DAY

May Day is an ancient festival marking the first day of summer. Throughout Europe, it's now also marked as a national holiday.

INGREDIENTS ▸ SERVES 6–8

- 75g CASTER SUGAR
- 100g SELF-RAISING FLOUR
- 1–2 TABLESPOON POPPY SEEDS or DESSICATED COCONUT
- ½ TEASPOON BAKING POWDER
- 2 EGGS
- 100g MARGARINE or BUTTER: melted
- 25ml MILK
- 1 LEMON: zest and juice
- 100g ICING SUGAR

HOW TO MAKE

1. PREPARATION

Preheat the oven to gas 4 or 180c (fan 160c).

You will need a 17cm lined round cake tin or a savarin tin.

2. DRY INGREDIENTS

Measure out all the dry ingredients into a bowl: sugar, flour, poppy seeds or desiccated coconut, baking powder and stir.

3. MAKE THE WET MIXTURE

Crack the eggs into a jug and give them a whisk with a fork.

Pour in the melted margarine and the milk and stir.

4. MAKE THE CAKE

Pour the wet mixture all over the dry ingredients and mix well so it is all combined.

Stir in the lemon zest only.

Make sure all the ingredients are coated with the wet mixture and no dry mixture can be seen.

Pour the mixture into your cake or savarin tin.

5. BAKE

Place the cake in the preheated oven for 20–30 minutes.

6. ICING

Whilst the cakes are baking, prepare the icing.

Juice the lemon and remove all the pips.

Place the icing sugar in a bowl and add a teaspoon of juice at a time, you want to make a white glossy icing.

7. DECORATE

Once the cake is cooled, pour over the flavoured icing.

VARIATIONS

Leave out the poppy seeds/desiccated coconut and have plain.

Make in mini loaf tins or a loaf tin.

Toast some coconut and sprinkle on the icing.

Crush up some pistachios and sprinkle on the icing.

Use an orange for a different flavour.

J

FATHER'S DAY MEDALS

June is when Father's Day occurs in the UK, but it is celebrated at different times of the year around the globe. Make a 'medal' for your dad or someone special!

INGREDIENTS ▸ MAKES 12

150g PLAIN FLOUR

100g BUTTER: leave in the fridge until needed

¼ TEASPOON BAKING POWDER

75g CASTER SUGAR

1 EGG YOLK

½ TEASPOON VANILLA ESSENCE

50–75g COLOURED FONDANT ICING

1 TABLESPOON OF JAM or LEMON CURD

HOW TO MAKE

1. PREPARATION

Preheat the oven to gas 5 or 190c (fan 170c).

Line a baking tray with greaseproof paper.

You will need a 7cm round cutter and a smaller round or shaped cutter plus some ribbon.

2. MAKE THE DOUGH

Place the flour into a bowl.

Chop the butter into cubes and add it to the flour.

Pick up some flour and butter and rub it between your hands. Keep rubbing the mixture between your fingertips until it starts to look like breadcrumbs.

TIP: Lift your hands out of the bowl as you rub, so the dough doesn't get sticky.

Stir in the baking powder and sugar.

3. CRACK

Crack the egg into a jug. Scoop out the yolk with half a shell or a tablespoon and add the yolk to the crumbed mixture. Pour in the vanilla essence.

Give it a mix with a spoon, then use your hands to pull it all together.

4. MATHS

Cut the ball of dough in half, and then in half again – you now have 4 pieces the same size.

Break each of the 4 pieces in half now – you now have 8 pieces of dough.

5. MEDALS

Sprinkle some flour on the table, place one piece of dough on the flour, sprinkle more flour on the top.

Very gently roll this piece of dough to 4mm in thickness. Cut out a circle.

Repeat with all the other pieces of dough.

Squeeze the leftover dough together and keep making medals until it runs out.

Place the medals onto a baking tray, leaving a little space between them.

Using the end of a teaspoon, make a hole near the top of each medal, large enough for a ribbon to be threaded through once they are baked.

TIP: Make sure the hole is wide enough as the medals will grow and the hole can close up.

6. BAKE

Place in the preheated oven for 12-15 minutes.

Take out and leave to cool on the baking tray.

7. DECORATE

Once cooled, thread through some ribbon, long enough so it will hang as a medal.

Divide your icing in half, sprinkle some icing sugar on the worktop and roll out each piece. Cut a smaller circle or shape you have chosen to go on your medal then using a little jam or lemon curd as your food glue, stick the shape onto the biscuit.

J F M A M **J J** A S O N D

STRAWBERRY SHORTBREAD

GAME! SET! MATCH! Yes, it's that time of year. Wimbledon! We need strawberries and cream so let's whizz up some shortbread! Anyone for tennis?

INGREDIENTS ▸ MAKES 8–15

- 100g BUTTER
- 50g CASTER SUGAR
- 125g PLAIN FLOUR
- 25g CORNFLOUR
- 1 TEASPOON VANILLA ESSENCE
- STRAWBERRIES: to serve
- CLOTTED or WHIPPED CREAM

HOW TO MAKE

1. PREPARATION

Preheat the oven to gas 4 or 180c (fan 160c).

Line a baking tray with greaseproof paper.

You will need a round cutter 4–6cm.

2. CREAM

Place the butter in a bowl and soften with the back of a spoon.

Add the sugar and mix until it sticks to the bowl.

3. FLOUR

Put the plain flour and cornflour in a bowl and mix together.

Add 2 tablespoons of the flour mix at a time to the butter and sugar. Mix together.

Repeat until all the flour mix is used up.

TIP: If you add the flour all at once the mixture will become crumbly.

Add in the vanilla essence.

Using your hands bring the mixture together to form a ball of dough.

TIP: If you have 30 minutes to spare, chill the dough, so the butter will solidify and make a firm shortbread, so they don't spread too much.

4. MATHS

Cut the ball of dough in half, and then in half again – you now have 4 pieces the same size.

5. FLOUR

Sprinkle some flour onto the worktop.

Place 1 of the pieces of shortbread dough on the flour.

Shake a little more flour over the top.

Gently roll the dough to ½cm in thickness.

TIP: Do not be heavy handed; the dough is fragile.

Take your cutter and cut out your rounds.

Add your leftovers to one of the other pieces, roll out again and keep repeating the process until you run out of dough!

Place the rounds onto a baking tray.

6. BAKE

Place in the preheated oven and bake for 15-18 minutes.

Take out and leave to cool on the baking tray.

TIP: Shortbread is pale in colour, so it won't be golden when it comes out.

7. STRAWBERRIES!

Once cooled, slice up some strawberries and place them on half of the shortbreads with some cream.

Place a shortbread biscuit on top.

KEY LIME PIE

INDEPENDENCE DAY

The 4th of July marks the day in 1776 when America declared political separation from Great Britain, and many festivities take place on this public holiday. Key lime pie is a favourite from the Florida Keys, but it is now found all over America and the rest of the world.

INGREDIENTS ▸ SERVES 4

150g DIGESTIVE BISCUITS

75g MARGARINE: melted

100g FULL FAT CREAM CHEESE

100ml DOUBLE CREAM

1 TIN CONDENSED MILK (397g)

2 LIMES: zest and juice

1–2 TABLESPOONS BOTTLED LIME JUICE

CHOCOLATE: grated

HOW TO MAKE

1. PREPARATION

You will need 4 small ramekin dishes or a round 15–18cm dish.

2. CRUSH

Place the biscuits into a bag or bowl.

Using the end of a rolling pin, crush up the biscuits. They should look like sand on a beach.

TIP: Make sure all the air is out of the bag and tie the bag up, before you start to crush them.

Pour the crushed biscuits into a bowl.

3. MIX

Pour the melted margarine over the crushed-up biscuits and stir.

Put the mixture into your serving dish(es), pressing the biscuits down with a spoon for an even spread.

Place in the fridge.

4. FILLING

Pour the cream cheese and double cream into a bowl.

Whisk them together until they go thick.

Stir in the condensed milk.

5. ZEST & JUICE

Wash the limes and dry.

Using the smallest holes on the grater, zest the lime.

TIP: The zest is a thin layer around the lime, so don't grate to the white, you should just have around a teaspoon of zest.

Now juice both limes, making sure you throw away any pips.

6. WHISK

Pour the juice and zest into the cream mixture.

Whisk together. The juice from the limes should start to thicken the mixture.

TIP: If it isn't thickening, add a spoonful from the bottle (this could be because the limes are small).

7. FINAL TOUCHES

Take the biscuit mixture out of the fridge.

Pour the creamy mixture all over the biscuit base, spreading it all over.

Sprinkle grated chocolate over the top.

Leave in the fridge for 2–3 hours to set.

VARIATIONS

Use chocolate-coated digestives or hob nobs for a chocolatey base.

Use 1 lemon and 1 lime.

Not sure what to do with the rest of the condensed milk and cream? See the kulfi ice-cream on page 74.

CHAUSSONS AUX POMMES

BASTILLE DAY

The 14th of July is Bastille Day in France, marking the start of the French Revolution. It is said the chaussons aux pommes date back to 1630, when a lady of the town distributed apples and flour to the poor and they baked apple turnovers.

INGREDIENTS ▸ MAKES 6

- **2 EATING APPLES**
- **1 TABLESPOON BUTTER**
- **1 TABLESPOON SOFT BROWN SUGAR**
- **1 TEASPOON CINNAMON**: optional
- **1 PACK of READY ROLLED PUFF PASTRY**
- **1 EGG WHITE**: for glazing
- **2 TABLESPOONS GRANULATED SUGAR**: for decoration

HOW TO MAKE

1. PREPARATION

Preheat the oven to gas 6 or 200c (fan 180c).

Wash the apples.

You will need a frying pan.

Line a baking tray with greaseproof paper.

2. CHOPPING

Cut the apples in half, then in half again, take out the core; then slice them into thin pieces.

3. COOK

Place the butter into a saucepan.

Add in the apple slices and the sugar. If you are using the cinnamon, add this too.

Place the saucepan on a low heat and cook the apples for 5–10 minutes, stirring occasionally.

4. PASTRY

Take the pastry from the packet and unroll it.

Flour the worktop and turn the pastry onto it.

Cut the pastry down the middle (lengthways).

Each length cut into 3 squares, so you have 6 squares for your apple turnovers.

TIP: To make a square, fold a corner to corner, this will mark where the square needs to be cut.

5. FILL

Place a tablespoon of the apple mixture into the centre of the pastry square.

Fill a cup half full of water. Dip your finger into the water.

Dab your finger round the edges of the pastry and fold over to create a triangle.

TIP: Don't dab too much water around the edges, otherwise the pastry will be too soggy to seal.

Using your finger or a fork, seal the triangles nice and tight, so the mixture will not leak out.

Place them on a baking tray.

6. READY TO COOK

Use a knife to make a hole in the top of the triangles to let the steam escape.

Using a pastry brush, brush them with egg white and sprinkle over some granulated sugar.

Place in the preheated oven for 15–20 minutes. Leave to cool.

VARIATIONS

Add some blackberries or other soft fruits.

Use 2 apples and some mincemeat for some Christmas puffs.

Use squares of chocolate instead of the apples inside for tasty chocolate puffs (the 7th of July is World Chocolate Day).

J J A

FESTIVAL FLAPJACK

Summer is a season with many festivals and it's nice when going out to take something to eat that won't melt but will fill you up. This flapjack is good for all of those things.

INGREDIENTS ▸ MAKES 9

75g MARGARINE

3 TABLESPOONS GOLDEN SYRUP

225g PORRIDGE OATS

75g GRANULATED SUGAR

100g DRIED APRICOTS: chopped

HOW TO MAKE

1. PREPARATION

Preheat the oven to gas 4 or 180c (fan 160c).

You will need an 18cm lined cake tin or tray bake tin.

2. MELT

Place the margarine and syrup in a heatproof bowl. Put the bowl in the microwave for 20–30 seconds to melt. Leave to cool.

TIP: If you haven't got a microwave, you can put the margarine and syrup in a pan and melt them on a low heat on the hob.

3. COMBINE

Place the oats, sugar and chopped apricots into bowl and mix them together with your hands.

Pour over the melted syrup and margarine, stir them together with a spoon.

4. BAKE

Spread the mixture into your lined tin.

Flatten it down with the back of a spoon to cover the tin.

Place it in the preheated oven for 20–25 minutes.

Once it comes out, leave for 10 minutes then cut into squares.

Leave to cool in the baking tray before taking the squares out.

VARIATIONS

To reduce the sugar, replace 25g of it with a mashed up banana and add in with the melted ingredients.

Replace some of the oats for desiccated coconut, seeds or nuts.

J F M A M J J A S O N D

CAMPING S'MORES

These delicious biscuits originated in summer holiday camps in America. The children would ask for 'some more' and said it so quickly and eagerly that it sounded like 's'more!'

INGREDIENTS ▸ MAKES 4

- 8 DIGESTIVE BISCUITS
- 8 SQUARES OF CHOCOLATE
- PACK of MINI MARSHMALLOWS

HOW TO MAKE

1. PREPARATION

You will need some foil to wrap the s'mores in.

2. BUILD

Lay the digestive biscuits flat on a worktop.

Place 2 squares of chocolate in the middle of 4 of the biscuits.

Place mini marshmallows all the way around the squares of chocolate.

Lay the remaining 4 digestives on top of each of the chocolate ones.

Wrap each one carefully in foil.

3. BAKE

Place in a campfire or a warm oven for 5 minutes.

VARIATIONS

Use chocolate coated digestives.

Add a chunk of Mars Bar for a gooey centre.

Use an ice cream cone: fill with chocolate and mini marshmallows, wrap in foil and bake the same.

Fire door
Keep
locked
shut

Build
Mrs Bun the Bak

Place
the Baker

Fancy!

Melt!

J F M A M J J **A** S O N D

PASTA CANNELLONI

FERRAGOSTO

In Italy, August the 15th is a public holiday. Ferragosto originated as a day off for the peasants and was the idea of Emperor Augustus. Usually, families get together for a big lunch and there are fireworks in some towns. The Buns remember going to see friends in Italy; we went down to the beach and then had a big feast at their house.

INGREDIENTS ▸ SERVES 4

PASTA

- 100g PLAIN FLOUR
- 1 EGG

FILLING

- 1 HANDFUL of SPINACH
- 2 SPRING ONIONS
- 3–4 SLICES of HAM: optional
- 1 PEPPER
- 75g MOZZARELLA
- 125g RICOTTA
- 200g TINNED TOMATOES
- FRESH BASIL
- 2–3 TABLESPOONS CRÈME FRAICHE
- 2–3 TABLESPOONS CHEESE: grated

HOW TO MAKE

1. PREPARATION

Preheat the oven to gas 5 or 190c (fan 170c).

You will need an ovenproof dish for the pasta 20 x 16cm.

2. MAKE THE PASTA

Place the flour into a bowl.

Crack the egg into a cup, make sure there is no shell and pour it into the flour.

Stir them together with a spoon.

You will need to use your hands to pull the mixture all together.

If you have a few crumbs add a little water and mix in.

Knead the dough for 5 minutes.

Leave the dough to rest, while you make the filling.

3. FILLING

Use your hands to tear the spinach into small pieces.

Using scissors, cut up the spring onions.

If using ham, tear it up with your hands.

Cut the pepper into long strips, then use scissors to cut the strips into smaller pieces.

Place all these ingredients into a bowl.

Tear in the mozzarella and add in the ricotta. Use a spoon and mix it all together.

It should all stick together to form a ball.

Divide

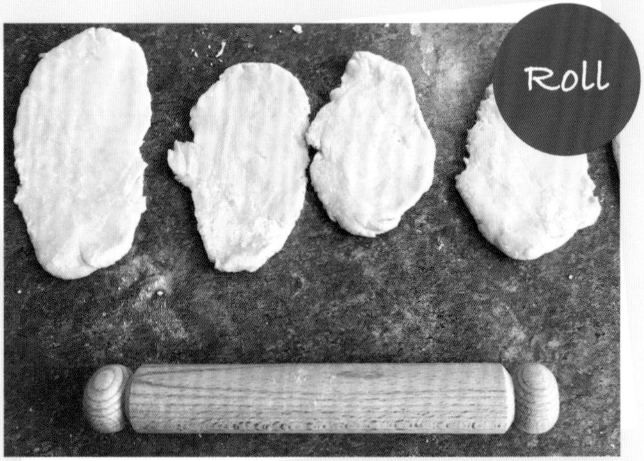
Roll

Fill

Place

Cover

Cheese

4. RECTANGLES

Divide the pasta dough into 6 equal pieces.

On a floured surface, roll each piece of dough into a rectangle shape about 15 x 10cm.

5. ROLLING

Share the filling evenly between the 6 rectangles of pasta.

Place a spoonful(s) at the end of each rectangle and spread it from end to end. Then roll it up.

Continue to fill and roll each piece.

Place the rolls into your ovenproof dish.

6. COVER

Pour over the tinned tomatoes.

Tear over the basil leaves.

Spread over the crème fraiche.

Sprinkle with the grated cheese.

7. BAKE

Place in the preheated oven for 20–30 minutes.

VARIATIONS

If you lack time, use fresh lasagne sheets as they work just as well.

Try using other vegetables.

Maybe try adding some cooked chicken?

If you can't eat gluten, use strips of courgette or aubergine instead of the pasta.

S

WHEATSHEAF

HARVEST FESTIVAL

Harvest Festival is a celebration of food grown on the land. When I was at school, we'd take food in during September to make up baskets to give to the local people. One year we made this at school. I loved combining design and baking.

INGREDIENTS

400g STRONG FLOUR

100g SPELT or WHOLEMEAL FLOUR

PINCH OF SALT

PINCH OF SUGAR

7g or 1 SACHET YEAST: fast action

250ml WARM WATER

1 EGG and 1 TABLESPOON MILK (mixed): for the glaze

HOW TO MAKE

1. PREPARATION

Preheat the oven to gas 6 or 200c (fan 180c).

You will need a baking tray.

2. DOUGH

Place the strong and spelt flour into the same bowl.

Add the salt and sugar on one side of the bowl.

Place the yeast on the other side of the bowl.

Run the tap until you have some warm water. Measure 250ml into a jug.

Pour the water into the flour and mix well until you have a ball of dough.

TIP: It isn't a soft dough; it will feel firm. This is because we want to shape it.

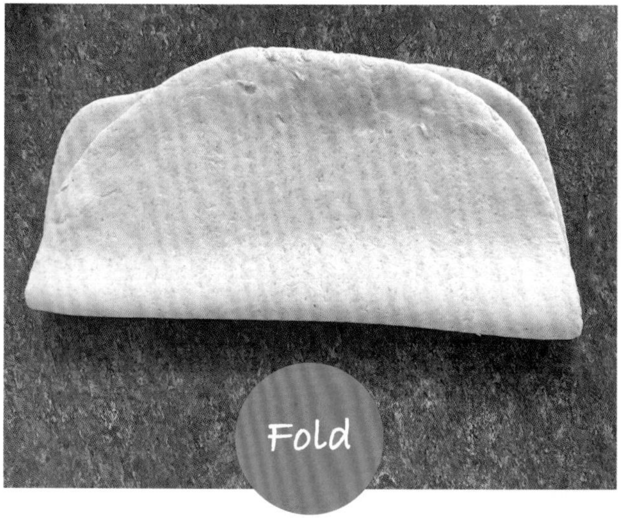

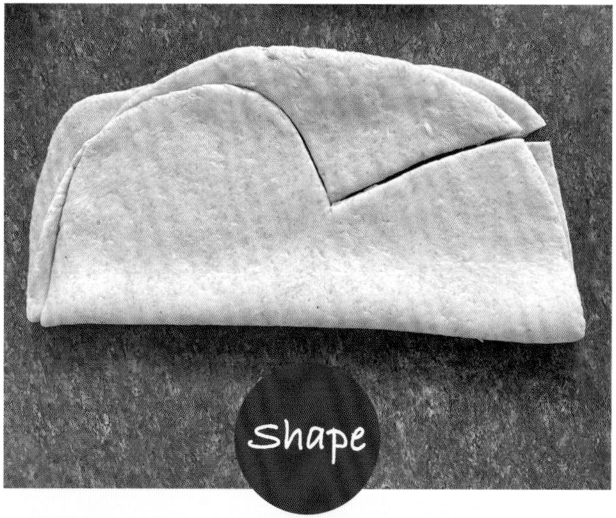

3. KNEAD & REST

Knead the dough on the worktop for 5 minutes.

Place the dough back into the bowl and cover with cling film.

Place in a warm place for 45–60 minutes to prove.

4. MATHS

Once the dough has proved, squash and squeeze the air out that has been created.

Cut the dough in half, so you have 2 equal pieces. Roll one piece into a rectangle 30 x 25cm.

TIP: Because the dough is firmer than a pizza dough you may not need any flour.

Fold it in half length ways, and cut out the shape of half a mushroom, then unfold it and you will have a large mushroom!

Add the leftovers to the other piece of dough.

Place the mushroom on a baking tray, prick it all over with a fork and brush with water.

TIP: The water will stop it drying out.

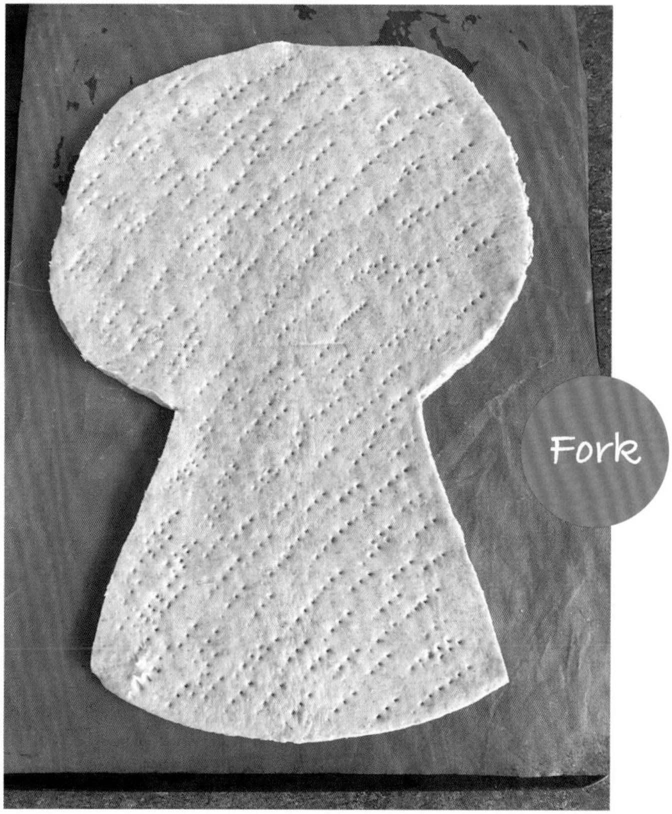

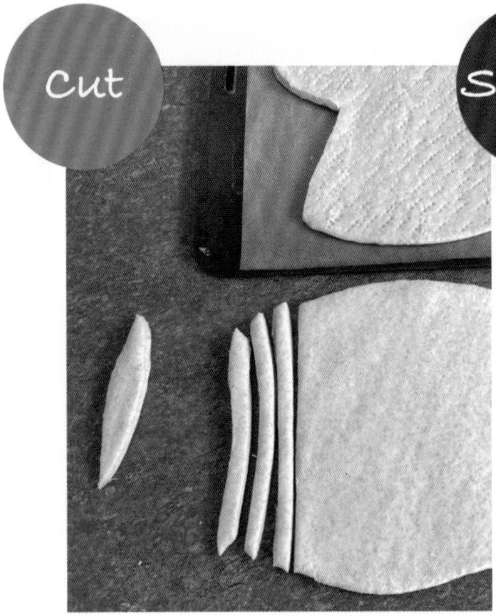

5. STEMS

Cut the other dough ball in half. Leave half to one side.

Roll the other half into a rectangle 30 x 17cm. (Sprinkle flour on the worktop if you need to.)

Cut it into 40 strips. (Keep 6 separate, so you will have 34 to use.)

Lay these onto the base of the mushroom to make the wheat stalks.

6. EARS

With the remaining half, cut it in half again (2 pieces), in half again (4-pieces), and in half again (8 pieces).

Now cut all these in half, you will have 16 pieces!

Tear each one of the 16 pieces into 6 pieces. 96 pieces in total. Now roll each one into an oval.

Using some scissors, cut 3 slits into each oval to look like ears of wheat.

7. DESIGN

Starting on the edge, lay the ears around the edge of the mushroom top, then fill the middle

TIP: You will use around 30 on the edge.

8. GLAZE

Crack the egg into a jug, add the milk and mix with a fork.

Using a pastry brush paint the glaze all over the ears and stalks.

With the remaining 6 strips, roll them a little longer and use 3 to make a plait, then the other 3 to make another plait.

Place this over the wheat stalks, crossing them over. Glaze these too.

9. BAKE

Place in the preheated oven for 25 minutes.

Then turn the temperature down to gas 4 or 180c (fan 160c) and cook for another 5–10 minutes until golden brown.

Baked

J F M A M J J A S O N D

BACK TO SCHOOL BISCUITS

These biscuits are great to make and bake and pop in your lunchbox. Choose from dinosaurs, fairies, animals or flowers. You can make them at Christmas too and turn a gingerbread man into a reindeer!

INGREDIENTS ▸ MAKES 20–30

75g PLAIN FLOUR

150g SELF-RAISING FLOUR

75g BUTTER

75g SOFT BROWN SUGAR

1 TEASPOON of GINGER or VANILLA ESSENCE

1 EGG

1 TABLESPOON SYRUP

DECORATIONS: icings, sprinkles, silver balls, chocolate or just leave plain

HOW TO MAKE

1. PREPARATION

Preheat the oven to gas 4 or 180c (fan 160c).

Line 2 baking trays with greaseproof paper.

Collect the cutters you would like to use.

2. MAKE THE DRY MIX

Place the plain and self-raising flour into the same bowl.

Chop the butter into cubes and add it to the flour.

Rub, rub, rub the butter into the flour with your fingertips until the mixture looks like breadcrumbs.

Add in the sugar and ginger or vanilla; stir it all together.

3. MAKE THE WET MIX

Crack the egg into a jug and beat with a fork.

Measure the syrup into the egg and mix well.

4. MAKE THE DOUGH

Now add the wet mixture to the dry mixture and stir well.

Use your hands to bring the mixture all together.

TIP: If you have time, wrap the dough in some cling film and place in the fridge for 30 minutes to chill. This will make it easier to roll out.

5. BISCUIT MAKING

Flour the worktop and split the dough into 4 pieces.

Place one piece on the flour and sprinkle some flour on the top.

Very gently roll this piece to the thickness of a pound coin.

Take your cutters and cut out your shapes.

Add your leftovers to one of the other 3 pieces, roll out again, and keep repeating the process until you run out of dough!

Place the shapes on the baking trays.

6. BAKE

Place in the preheated oven and bake for 20 minutes.

TIP: If the shapes are different sizes, they won't all require the same cooking time, so bake smaller biscuits together (for example on different baking trays). This way the biscuits shouldn't burn.

Take out of the oven and leave to cool on the baking tray.

7. DECORATE

Once cooled, decorate any way you like – no two need ever be the same!

VARIATIONS

This recipe can be used for any celebration – just change the cutters.

J F M A M J J A **S** **O** N D

ONION CAKE

ZWIEBELKUCHEN FESTIVAL

Mrs Bun's nephew is living in southern Germany. He told me all about Zwiebelkuchen Festival that takes place in the autumn. A whole festival just to celebrate an onion cake which is held in many of the villages around where he lives.

INGREDIENTS ▸ SERVES 4

DOUGH

- 200g STRONG FLOUR
- 1 TEASPOON or ½ SACHET YEAST: fast action
- 120ml COLD WATER
- 20g MARGARINE

FILLING

- 450–500g ONIONS: 4-5 medium onions
- 1 TABLESPOON BUTTER
- 75g HAM or COOKED BACON: chopped
- 2 EGGS
- 110ml DOUBLE CREAM or CRÈME FRAICHE
- SEASONING
- PINCH NUTMEG
- 50g CHEDDAR CHEESE: grated

HOW TO MAKE

1. PREPARATION

Preheat the oven to gas 5 or 190c (fan 170c).

You will need an 18cm ovenproof round dish and a frying pan.

2. MAKE THE DOUGH

Place the flour into a bowl.

Add the yeast and stir together.

Measure 120ml cold water into a jug.

Pour the water into the flour, add the margarine and stir it all together with a spoon until you have a ball of dough.

TIP: You will need to use your hands to bring the dough all together.

3. KNEADING

Knead the dough for 5 minutes on a floured surface.

Leave the dough to rest whilst you prepare the filling.

4. ONIONS

Using a sharp knife cut the tops off all the onions, now peel the coats off them.

Cut through the onion's root; you will have 2 halves.

TIP: Just cutting the top off means the onion will stay together and not fall apart.

Slice each half into strips; they will look like the arcs of a rainbow.

5. SOFTEN

Place a tablespoon of butter in the frying pan and add in the onions.

Turn the hob onto a LOW heat; we are just softening the onions.

TIP: If the heat is too high the onions will just burn.

Cook the onions for 10 minutes, stirring occasionally.

Add in the bacon or ham, stir and turn off the hob. Leave it to one side.

6. CRACK THE EGGS

Crack the eggs into a jug.

TIP: To crack the egg, tap it lightly on a table. If it's not cracked, have another go, but not too hard!

Pour in the double cream or crème fraiche. Whisk them together with a fork.

Add some seasoning and a pinch of nutmeg.

7. COMBINE

Pour the eggs over the onions and bacon or ham.

8. ROLL, ROLL, ROLL

Place the dough on a lightly floured surface, and using your rolling pin, roll into a circle to fit your dish.

TIP: If the dough doesn't seem to be getting bigger, make some fingerprints in it and use the rolling pin to flatten them and the dough will grow.

Place the dough into your dish. Use your fingers to push the dough up the sides of the ovenproof dish.

9. POUR & FILL

Pour in the onion filling and sprinkle over the grated cheese.

10. BAKE

Place in the preheated oven for 25–30 minutes.

Dough

Fill

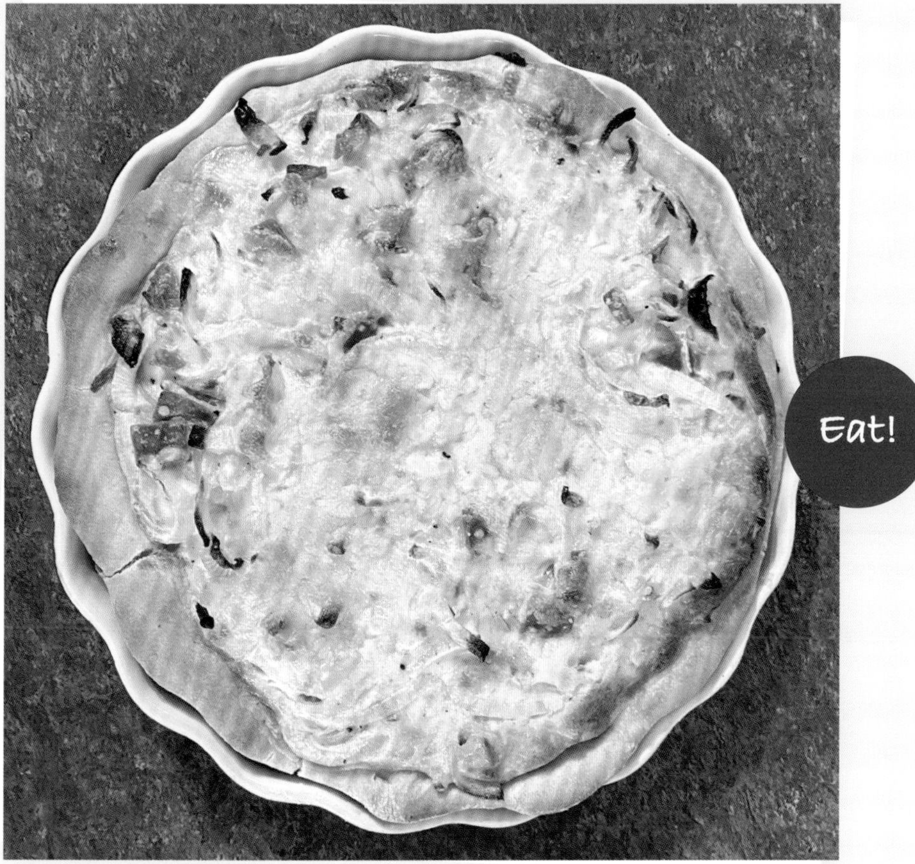
Eat!

J F M A M J J A S **O** N D

CINNAMON BUNS

KANELBULLENS DAG

Started in in Sweden in 1999, the 4th of October celebrates the many Swedish buns (kanelbullens). If you're not too sure about cinnamon buns, why not try the chocolate version in the variation overleaf.

INGREDIENTS ▸ MAKES 8

DOUGH

- 150ml MILK
- 25g BUTTER
- 250g STRONG FLOUR
- 1 TEASPOON or ½ SACHET YEAST: fast action
- 1 TABLESPOON BROWN SUGAR

FILLING

- 35g BUTTER
- 2 TEASPOONS BROWN SUGAR
- 2 TEASPOONS CINNAMON

HOW TO MAKE

1. PREPARATION

Preheat the oven to gas 5 or 190c (fan 170c).

You will need an ovenproof round 18cm dish.

2. WET & DRY

Pour the milk into a heatproof bowl, add the butter and place in the microwave for 20 seconds or until the butter has melted and the mixture is warm.

Place the flour into a bowl, add the yeast and sugar, mix it through with your hands or a spoon.

3. COMBINE

Pour the warm milk mixture over the dry ingredients.

Stir them together with a spoon until it is all combined, then bring it together with your hands.

TIP: If it is too dry add a little more milk, too wet add some more flour.

4. KNEAD & ROLL

Knead the dough on the worktop for 5 minutes.

TIP: Kneading is the stretching, pushing, folding and pressing of your dough in order to make it rise.

Sprinkle the worktop with some flour and place the dough on top.

Sprinkle a little more flour over the top and roll the dough out into a rectangle 30 x 20cm.

TIP: Make fingerprints in the dough, then use your rolling pin to iron them out and watch the dough grow!

5. PAINT

Mix the butter, sugar and cinnamon up together in a cup then have a taste test. More sugar? Cinnamon?

Use a knife to spread the mixture all over the rolled-out dough, right up to the edges.

6. ROLL UP! ROLL UP!

Take the longest side and tuck it in slightly and start rolling it up.

You should have a long Swiss-roll or sausage shape.

7. MATHS

Cut the roll in half, so you have 2 pieces, then cut each roll in half again so you have 4 pieces.

Now cut each one in half again, so you have 8 pieces.

TIP: Saw through rather than pushing down with the knife; this will make the rolls rounder.

Place them ring side up around the ovenproof dish. Or, in a flower shape: one cinnamon bun in the middle with 7 around it.

Cover with some cling film and leave in a warm place to rise for 45–60 minutes.

8. BAKE

Place in the preheated oven for 20–25 minutes until golden brown and hollow at the bottom when tapped.

VARIATIONS

CHOCOLATE BUNS

100g CHOCOLATE CHIPS

25g BUTTER

2 TABLESPOONS COCOA

1 TABLESPOON ICING SUGAR

Melt all the ingredients together then spread it all over the dough with a knife.

Roll and cook the same as above.

Eat!

APPLE PIE

APPLE DAY

Apple Day is celebrated on the 21st of October and began in the 1990s. Did you know there are apples with names like Jazz, Kanzi, Rubens, Cox and Discovery! This apple pie is one Great Grandma Bun used to make. She made the BEST apple pie, but left no written recipe behind, so my recipe is from memory. Every time I make it, it tastes more and more like hers.

INGREDIENTS ▸ SERVES 6

PASTRY

- 250g PLAIN FLOUR
- 125g BUTTER
- 2 TABLESPOONS CASTER SUGAR
- 3–5 TABLESPOONS of COLD WATER

FILLING

- 3–4 BRAMLEY APPLES: you can also use eating apples or a mix of both
- 3–4 TABLESPOONS SUGAR
- CINNAMON: optional
- 1 EGG WHITE: for glazing
- 1 TABLESPOON GRANULATED SUGAR: for decoration

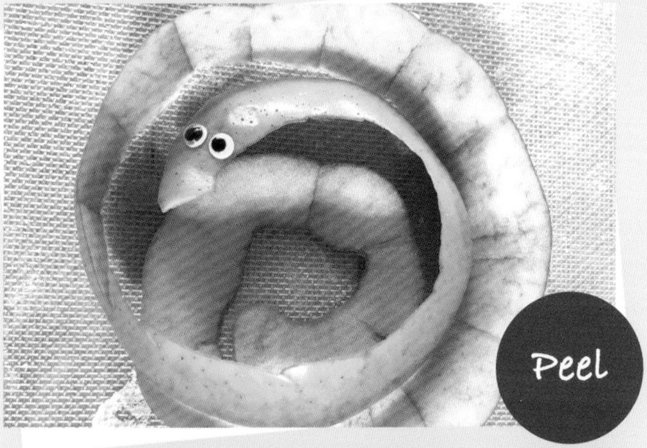

HOW TO MAKE

1. PREPARATION

Preheat the oven to gas 5 or 190c (fan 170c).

You will need a 16–18cm pie dish or 6 small dishes.

2. PASTRY

Place the flour into a bowl.

Chop the butter into cubes and add it to the flour.

Rub, rub, rub the butter into the flour with your fingertips until the mix looks like breadcrumbs.

Now add the two tablespoons of sugar.

Measure in 4 tablespoons of cold water and squeeze the dough together. If it isn't sticking together, add a little more water.

TIP: Pastry likes to be cold; whilst you prepare the apples, place it in the fridge. This stops the pastry from shrinking when baking.

3. APPLES

Wash the eating apples.

If you are using bramley apples they will need to be peeled. Eating apples don't need to be peeled unless you want to.

4. SLICE

Cut the apples in half and then in half again so you have 4 quarters.

You will need to take the core out of them and then slice thinly.

TIP: To stop the apples browning (oxidation) whilst you slice the others, place the slices in a bowl of water.

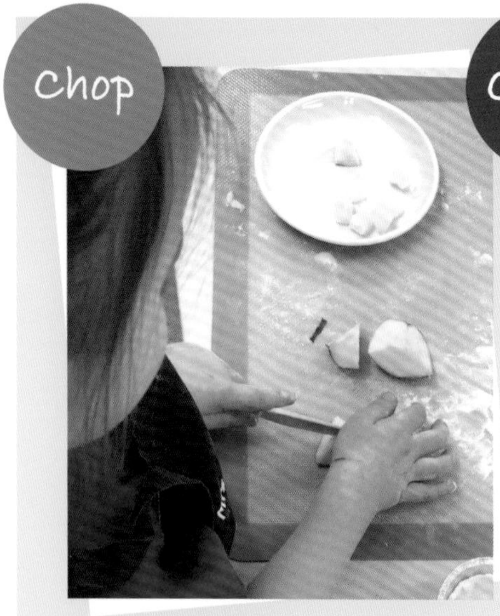

5. COLD PASTRY

Take the pastry out of the fridge.

Cut it in half, with one piece a little bigger than the other.

Take the smaller piece.

Flour the worktop, place the smaller half on the flour, sprinkle a little more flour over the top.

Roll it out to fit the top of your pie dish, this will create the lid.

TIP: Place your dish on the pastry and cut round; you will then have the right size. (Put it to one side for later.)

Add the off cuts to your other piece and roll it out to fit the pie dish bottom.

TIP: Keep turning the pastry as you roll it, to get a circle rather than an oval.

Place the pastry you have just rolled into the bottom of the pie dish. Cut off any overhanging pastry.

TIP: With these extra bits, make some pastry shapes to go on top of the pie.

6. FILL AND TOP

Drain the sliced apples and sprinkle over the sugar and cinnamon if using. Mix through with your hands.

Layer the apple slices up inside the pastry case, until they are all gone.

Brush the edge of the pastry lid with some egg or milk, then place on top.

Go round with a fork to seal the edges and make a hole in the middle to let some steam escape.

Using a pastry brush, paint the lid with egg white and sprinkle with some sugar.

7. BAKE

Place in the preheated oven and bake for 25–40 minutes (depending on the size of your tin).

VARIATIONS

Do a lattice on the pie top or add letters or leaves to decorate it.

Add some blackberries with the apples.

Make a crumble topping instead of a pastry top (100g flour, 50g butter, 50g sugar).

J F M A M J J A S O N D

WITCH'S FINGERS

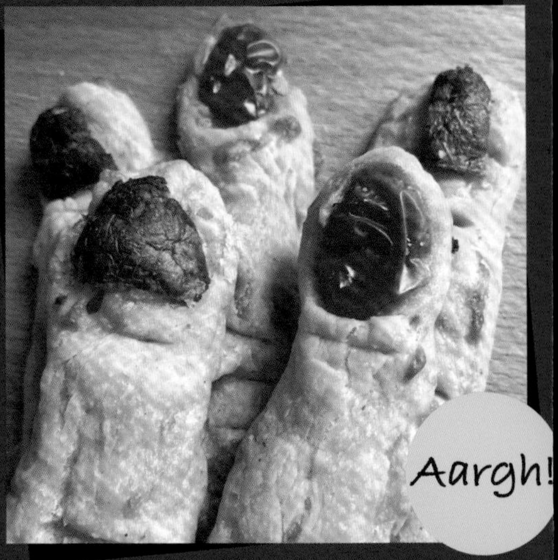

HALLOWEEN

A fun time of year to dress up, trick or treat and carve a pumpkin.

INGREDIENTS ▸ MAKES 10

110g PLAIN FLOUR

75g BUTTER or HARD MARGARINE: leave in the fridge until needed

75g CHEESE: grated (use a strong cheese for flavour)

2–3 TABLESPOONS MILK

1 TEASPOON GREEN PESTO: optional

FINGER-NAILS: sausage, pepper, ham, tomato, pepperoni

HOW TO MAKE

1. PREPARATION

Preheat the oven to gas 5 or 190c (fan 170c).

Line a baking tray with greaseproof paper.

2. MAKE THE DOUGH

Place the flour into a bowl.

Chop the butter into cubes and add it to the flour.

Pick up some flour and butter and rub it between your fingertips (as though you are trying to get rid of something that's stuck).

Keep rubbing the mixture between your fingertips until it starts to look like breadcrumbs.

Add the grated cheese.

Stir the teaspoon of pesto (if using) into the milk and mix well.

Slowly add this milk to the cheesy mixture and mix well with a spoon until it forms a soft ball.

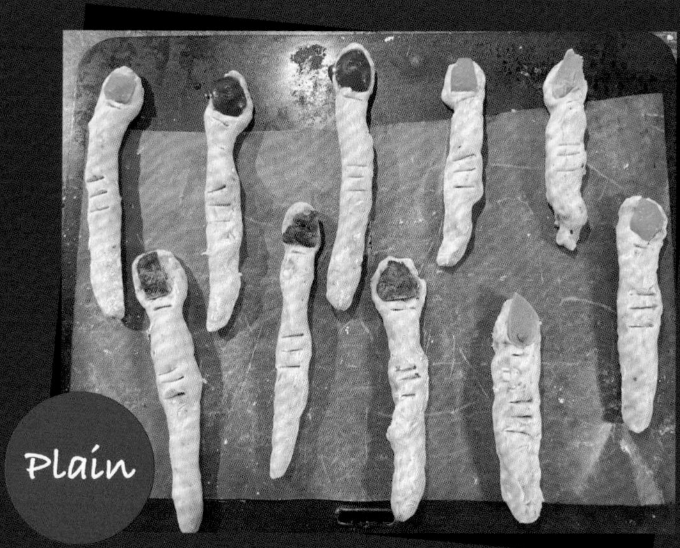

3. TAKE A BREAK

Give the ball of dough a good squeeze.

Place the dough back into the bowl and place in the fridge for 30 minutes to chill out.

4. MATHS

Cut the dough in half, then each half into 5 pieces. You now have 10 pieces in total.

Then each half is a hand! (5 pieces).

5. FINGERS

Take a piece of dough between your palm, roll it up and down to create a sausage shape (if it's a little sticky, flour your hands).

Roll all the pieces into 8 finger shapes and 2 thumbs, so you have 2 hands! Or all fingers!

TIP: They don't have to be all straight and the same size, you can have some short, long, bendy, knobbly... be an artist!

Place them on a baking tray, a little apart as they spread.

6. BAKE

Place them in the preheated oven for 15–18 minutes.

Remove from the oven, leave to cool for a couple of minutes, and then transfer to a cooling rack.

VARIATIONS

Flavour the mix with a sprinkle of paprika.

Add bits of spring onions or pepper to make warts on the fingers.

Add fresh herbs: parsley, chives to make green speckled fingers.

J F M A M J J A S O **N** D

MEXICAN BOWLS & GUACAMOLE

DAY OF THE DEAD

In Mexico, November the 1st & 2nd is a two-day holiday (Dia de los Muertos) where family and friends gathering to pray for and remember those who have passed away. Try these Mexican bowls and guacamole.

INGREDIENTS ▸ SERVES 4–6

GUACAMOLE

- 2 SPRING ONIONS
- 1 TOMATO
- 1 TABLESPOON SOUR CREAM
- 1–2 TEASPOON LEMON JUICE
- 1 AVOCADO
- SEASONING

MEXICAN BOWLS

- OIL: for painting
- 4–6 SMALL TORTILLA WRAPS
- 2 TOMATOES
- ½ PEPPER
- 50g GREEN BEANS: cooked
- 2–3 TABLESPOONS SWEETCORN: cooked
- 2–3 LETTUCE LEAVES
- 1 AVOCADO
- 1–2 TEASPOONS LEMON JUICE
- 2–3 SPRIGS of CORIANDER
- 4 TABLESPOONS REFRIED BEANS
- SOUR CREAM and CRESS

Yum!

HOW TO MAKE

1. PREPARATION

Preheat the oven to gas 4 or 180c (fan 160c).

You will need 4–6 small ovenproof ramekins.

2. PAINT

Using a pastry brush, dip it into the oil and paint one side of the tortilla wrap.

Place them, oil side down into the ramekins.

Place in the preheated oven for 8–10 minutes.

3. CHOP, CUT AND TEAR

Cut the tomatoes in half, then in half again, so you have 4 pieces. Use scissors to cut them into smaller pieces.

Cut the pepper into slices, then using scissors cut the strips into smaller pieces.

Chop the green beans into smaller pieces.

Place them all into a bowl and add in the sweetcorn.

Tear the lettuce leaves into small pieces and add to the other vegetables.

Cut around the avocado, give it a wiggle and it should come apart.

Take out the stone and scoop out the flesh with a spoon.

Cut it up into small pieces and add to the vegetables. Mix well.

4. SEASON

Drizzle with the lemon juice. Take the leaves off the coriander and tear them into the mixture.

5. FILL

Place a tablespoon of refried beans at the bottom of the cooked tortilla bowls. Spoon the vegetable filling over the top.

To serve add a spoonful of sour cream on top and a sprinkling of the cress.

GUACAMOLE

Using scissors, chop the spring onions up into small pieces.

Cut the tomato in half with a knife, and in half again then into small pieces and place into a bowl.

Stir in the sour cream and lemon juice.

Cut around the avocado, give it a wiggle and it should come apart. Take out the stone.

Mark criss-crosses into the avocado and push it inside out.

Use a fork to mash it up or use your hands and get really messy!

Add to the sour cream mixture, season. Eat!

N

MANGO KULFI

DIWALI

Starting on the 4th of November Diwali is a five-day festival of lights, celebrated by Hindus. There are feasts and many gifts are shared. This sweet treat, kulfi, sometime known as Indian ice-cream, is one of the treats you can eat.

INGREDIENTS ▸ MAKES 6–12 LOLLIES

400ml WHIPPING CREAM

200g CONDENSED MILK

200g EVAPORATED MILK

300g **MANGO**: fresh or tinned

GROUND PISTACHIOS: optional

HOW TO MAKE

1. PREPARATION

You will need 6 large or 12 small ice cream lolly moulds & lolly sticks.

2. WHISK

Pour the whipping cream into a bowl and whisk until thick. You will have to be strong to do this!

TIP: The cream will go from being runny to sticking to the whisk, looking like an ice cream!

Stir in the condensed and evaporated milks.

3. PURÉE

Peel the mango or drain it from the tin.

Using a knife, cut it up into smaller pieces.

Place it into a blender and whizz it up until you have a purée.

Add it into the milky mixture.

4. FREEZE

Sprinkle some crushed pistachios into the bottom of the lolly moulds (optional).

Pour the ice-cream mixture into your 6–12 lolly moulds.

Place your filled lolly moulds in the freezer.

Be patient! You will need to leave the lollies for at least 6 hours before you can eat them!

You can have a taste test of the mixture left in the bowl though!

TIP: When you're ready to eat them, run the lolly moulds under some warm water and it should loosen the lolly to come out.

VARIATIONS

Instead of puréeing the mango, mash it up and freeze in a large container, and serve as ice-cream.

For a pistachio flavour, crush pistachios into a dusty mixture and add to the cream mixture.

Add some cardamon to flavour.

Not sure what to do with the rest of the condensed milk and cream? See the Key lime pie recipe on page 38.

J F M A M J J A S O **N** D

BONFIRE BREAD

Remember, remember the 5th of November! Bonfires, fireworks and, of course, the gunpowder plot and the Houses of Parliament!

INGREDIENTS SERVES 3–6

- **200g STRONG FLOUR**
- **1 TEASPOON or ½ SACHET YEAST**: fast action
- **PINCH OF SALT**
- **120ml WARM WATER**
- **1 TABLESPOON OLIVE OIL**
- **75–100g CHEDDAR CHEESE**: grated
- **3–4 LARGE SAUSAGES**: cooked and sliced
- **1 LARGE or 4 SMALL TOMATOES**: chopped

HOW TO MAKE

1. PREPARATION

Preheat the oven to gas 6 or 200c (fan 180c).

You will need a 6 holed muffin tin or an 18cm round tin.

2. MAKE THE DOUGH

Place the flour into a bowl.

Stir in the yeast and salt.

Run the tap until you have some warm water. Measure 120ml into a jug and add the oil.

Pour the water and oil into the flour and mix well until you have a ball of dough.

3. KNEADING

Knead the dough for 5 minutes on a floured surface.

TIP: Kneading is the stretching, pushing, folding and pressing of your dough in order to make it rise.

4. ROLL OUT

Place the kneaded dough onto a lightly floured surface and roll it out to a rectangle 30 x 20cm.

TIP: Make fingerprints in the dough, then use your rolling pin to iron them out and watch the dough grow!

5. FILL

Sprinkle over the grated cheese, sliced sausages and chopped tomatoes all over the dough.

6. ROLL UP! ROLL UP!

Take the longest edge and tuck it in tightly and start rolling it up.

You should have a long Swiss-roll or sausage shape.

7. MATHS

Cut the roll in half, then each half into 3 pieces, so you have 6 pieces.

Place them ring side up into the muffin tray or the round tin.

Cover with some cling film and leave in a warm place to rise for 45–60 minutes.

8. BAKE

Place in the preheated oven for 18–25 minutes until golden brown and hollow at the bottom when tapped.

VARIATIONS

Fill with cheese and pickle for a picnic lunch.

Make a pizza roll: tomato, cheese and your favourite toppings, roll up and you have pizza rolls.

Add garlic butter, slice thinner and have garlic dough rolls.

LATKES

HANUKKAH

Hanukkah, the Jewish 'Festival of Lights', celebrates the liberation of the Holy Temple from the Greek army in the 2nd century BC. To rededicate the temple a lamp was lit with enough oil to last for 1 day – but it burned for 8. Latkes, fried in oil, are a staple of Hanukkah celebrations.

INGREDIENTS ▸ MAKES 6–8

275g POTATOES

1 SMALL ONION

1 EGG

1 TABLESPOON PLAIN FLOUR

OIL: for frying

HOW TO MAKE

1. PREPARATION

You will need a frying pan.

2. GRATING

Wash the potatoes, but no need to peel.

Cut larger potatoes in half.

Use the largest holes on the grater, to grate all the potatoes.

Cut the top off the onion and peel off the coat.

Cut through the onion's root so you have 2 pieces.

Grate the onion as you did the potato.

3. SQUEEZE

Place both the potato and onion into a tea-towel.

Then squeeze out as much water from them as you can.

Watch all the water drain out.

TIP: You need to get the potatoes and onions as dry as you possibly can, so keep squeezing!

4. MIX

Place the potato and onion mixture into a bowl.

Crack the egg into a jug, make sure there is no shell and pour it into the potato and onion mixture.

Add in the tablespoon of flour and mix well.

5. FRY

Pour a tablespoon of oil into the frying pan.

Scoop some mixture onto a tablespoon.

Place it in the frying pan, and depending how large the frying pan is, add a few more scoops.

Flatten them down with a spatula.

Fry on both sides on a low to medium heat for 2–3 minutes or until golden brown.

VARIATIONS

Use some parsnip instead of all potato.

Use some sweet potatoes.

Have a mix of root vegetables such as carrot, parsnip and potatoes!

J F M A M J J A S O N **D**

CHRISTMAS SCONES

There are so many amazing goodies to bake at Christmas! These scones are a twist on the traditional recipe we have for afternoon tea. But yes, we can still have them for a Christmas afternoon tea.

INGREDIENTS ▸ MAKES 6–8

- 250g PLAIN FLOUR
- 50g BUTTER
- 3 TABLESPOONS CASTER SUGAR
- 2½ TEASPOONS BAKING POWDER
- 25g SULTANAS
- 25g CRANBERRIES
- 50g WHITE CHOCOLATE CHIPS
- 1 TEASPOON MIXED SPICE: optional
- 1 EGG
- 75ml NATURAL YOGHURT

HOW TO MAKE

1. PREPARATION

Preheat the oven to gas 5 or 190c (fan 170c).

Line a baking tray with greaseproof paper.

You will need a 6cm cutter.

2. RUB, RUB, RUB

Place the flour into a bowl.

Chop the butter into cubes and add it to the flour.

Rub, rub, rub the butter into the flour with your fingertips until the mix looks like breadcrumbs.

Now add the 3 tablespoons of sugar and the baking powder.

3. FLAVOUR

Add in the sultanas, cranberries and white chocolate chips.

If you are using the mixed spice, add this in now. Stir it all together.

4. CRACK

Crack the egg into a jug and check there is no shell.

TIP: To crack the egg, tap it lightly on a table. If it's not cracked, have another go, but not too hard!

Add in the yoghurt and whisk them together with a fork.

5. MIX

Add the egg mixture to the flour mixture and stir well.

Use your hands to bring the mixture all together.

6. SCONE MAKING

Flour the worktop.

Press down the scone dough with your hands so it is 2–3cm thick.

TIP: You can use a rolling pin but be careful not to roll it out too thin, as you will end up with biscuits instead!

Take your cutter and cut out your scones.

Put the leftovers together, press down again and cut more scones.

7. BAKE

Place the scones on a baking tray, leaving space around them.

TIP: If they are too near together the sides of the scones don't crisp up.

Brush with some milk (optional).

Place in the preheated oven for 15–20 minutes until golden and risen.

VARIATIONS

Use all sultanas for a scone any time of the year!

Swap the fruit for cheese and leave out the sugar for a savoury scone. Try adding some chives.

CHRISTMAS PUDDING BISCUITS

These fun biscuits look just like mini Christmas puddings!

INGREDIENTS ▸ MAKES 12–15

- 125g MARGARINE
- 75g CASTER SUGAR
- 150g PLAIN FLOUR
- 25g COCOA POWDER
- 100g WHITE FONDANT ICING
- HOLLY ICING SHAPES
- WHITE CHOCOLATE CHIPS

HOW TO MAKE

1. PREPARATION

Preheat the oven to gas 5 or 190c (fan 170c).

Line a baking tray with greaseproof paper.

You will need a 6–7cm round cutter.

2. CREAM

Place the margarine in a bowl and soften it with the back of a spoon.

Add in the sugar and mix until it sticks to the bowl.

3. FLOUR

Pour in half the flour and give the mixture a stir.

Then add in the other half of the flour, with the cocoa powder and mix well.

Bring the dough together with your hands to form a ball.

TIP: Give it a good squeeze to make sure it is all chocolatey.

4. MATHS

Cut the ball of dough in half, and then each half in half again. You now have 4 pieces.

Sprinkle the worktop with some flour.

5. ROLL

Place one piece of dough onto the flour, sprinkle a little more flour over the top.

Roll it to a thickness of 3-4mm and cut out 2 circles.

Bring the leftovers together and roll out and cut circle number 3.

Repeat this with the other 3 pieces of dough, so you will have 12 biscuits.

Bring any leftover mixture together and cut out some extra biscuits.

Place the biscuits on the baking tray.

TIP: Remember how many went in!

6. BAKE

Place them in the preheated oven for 10–15 minutes.

Leave to cool.

7. DECORATE

Squash and squeeze the fondant icing to get it soft.

Sprinkle some icing sugar on the table and roll out the fondant icing.

Cut out circles, using the same size cutter as the biscuits.

Using the jagged edge of the cutter, cut 2 segments from the circle. This will give you the pudding icing for 2 biscuits.

Continue cutting the half circles until you have enough for the biscuits in the oven.

Once the biscuits are cooled use some jam to stick the pudding icing to the top of the biscuit.

Add some holly shaped icings and some white chocolate chips for pudding spots.

THANK YOU

I would like to thank so many of you wonderful people who are part of the Bun community, as without you, all this would not be possible. I love to create, make and bake with you, always trying something different in classes. Mr Bun and Son Bun, thank you for taste testing all my new recipes so they could pass through to the cookery class stage. Thanks for not tiring of yet another pasta dish, pie, cake or biscuit! There is always food in the Bun house...

Cookie Bun, thank you for the way you listen to me and never answer back! Brother Bun, thank you for your patience and understanding when working on the book with me. Big thanks to Grandma & Grandad Bun for reading through and offering advice, and Grandma Bun for the baking gene.

Jen, thank you for your red pen marking! Caroline Allington, thank you for the cover photograph of junior Bun chefs (left to right below), Rafe, Willow and Hunter.

All of your support is foodtastic!

hello@mrsbunthebaker.net
www.mrsbunthebaker.net

www.facebook.com/mrsbunthebaker
@AMrsbunthebaker mrsbunthebaker

ISBN 978-1-3999-0316-5